JOE AND
THE PIRATES

All inquiries should be addressed to:
BoggleNoggin Media Inc.
102 Dunant Crescent
Penticton, B.C.
Canada
V2A 3E9

www.bogglenoggin.com

ISBN: 978-1-897351-01-7
EAN: 9781897351017

Kate was reading a book.

"Joe," asked Kate, "do you know why ships don't tip over when the wind blows?"

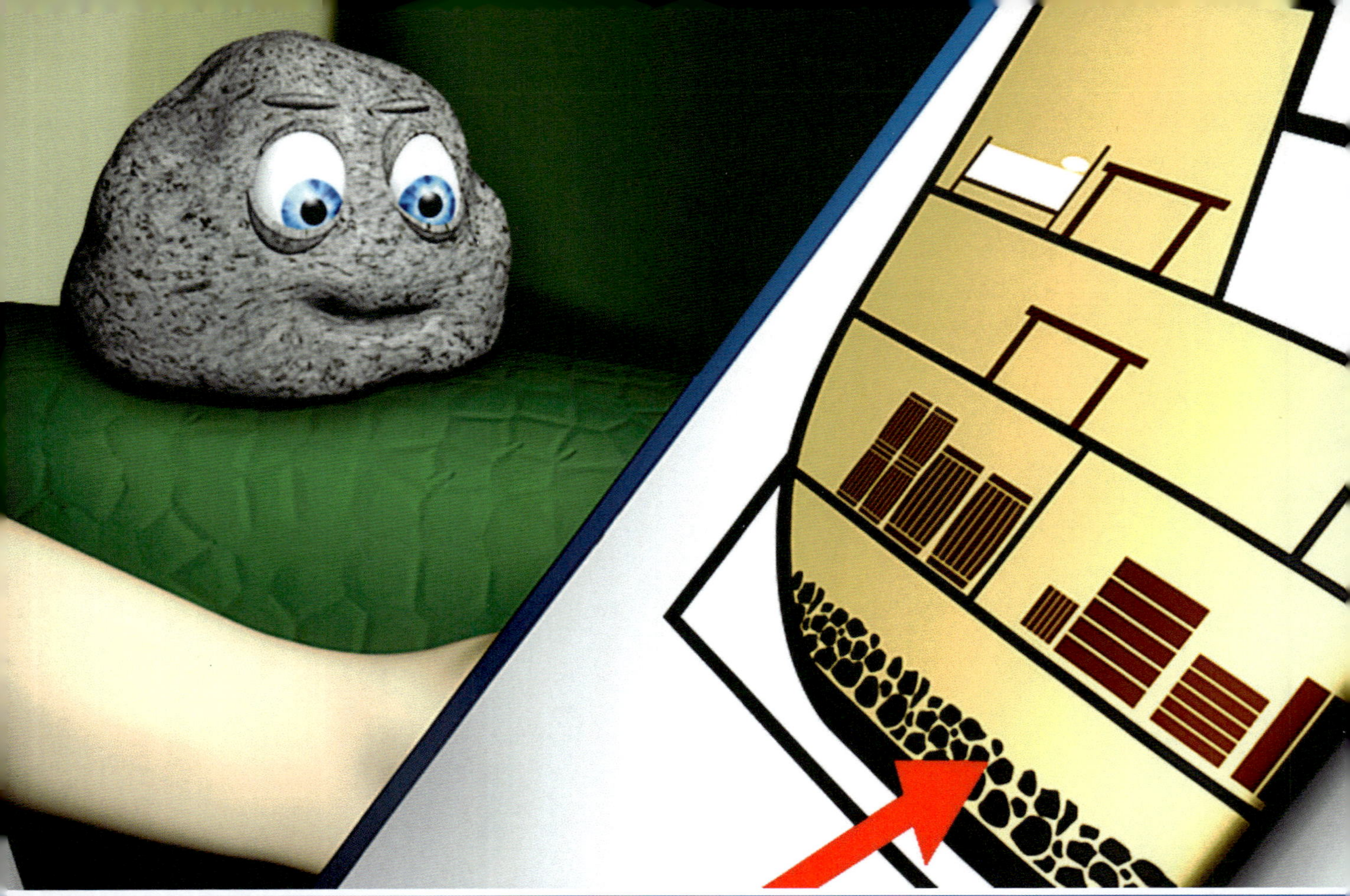

"Of course," answered Joe. "It's because they put lots of heavy rocks, like me, in the bottom of the ship. It's called ballast."

"Joe, is this one of your tall tales?" asked Kate.

"No, it's true," insisted Joe.

"I was part of the ballast once," bragged Joe. "I crossed the ocean in a sailing ship. We were attacked by pirates."

Kate had heard this story before, but she wanted to hear it again.

"Tell me," she said.

I had been laying on a sunny beach working on my tan. The next thing I knew, someone grabbed me.

They put me in the hold with some other rocks.

"The hold is the bottom of the ship," said Joe.

"I know," said Kate.

The hold was dark and smelly and wet. We were telling each other rock jokes to pass the time.

Suddenly, there was a loud shout from on deck.

"Ship ahoy . . . Pirates!" yelled someone. "It's the ship of Not-So-Scary Bob, the meanest pirate in the world."

There was a lot of running and shouting on deck as the sailors prepared to fight the pirates.

There was a huge noise as the cannons were fired.

Again and again the cannons were reloaded and fired.
There was lots of smoke.

Two sailors came down to the hold for more gunpowder.
One said, "The pirates have not hit us yet."
"They must be terrible shots," said the other.
They both laughed.

Then it grew very quiet on deck.

The cannons had stopped firing.

One of the crew yelled, "We're out of cannon balls, Captain."

A sailor came into the hold.

"This might work," he said and reached down and grabbed ME.

I was excited to go on deck and see the action.

"Captain, this one is perfect," reported the sailor.

"I hope he will save us," said the captain. "He is our only hope."

"Save us?" I thought. "Me? How?"

Then they put me in the cannon. It was dark and hot.

Someone yelled, "FIRE!"

I flew out of the cannon with my eyes shut tight.

When I opened my eyes, I was way up in the air, flying with some geese.

"Hello, Joe," they said. "Going south?"

I looked down.

I was falling toward the pirate ship. I was heading right for the captain.

With all the smoke from his cannons, he couldn't see that his ship was headed for some sharp rocks.

But I could.

I missed the captain but hit the ship's wheel and knocked it right out of his hands.

The wheel spun around, and the pirate ship suddenly turned.

I bounced into a barrel of fish.

Did MY ship escape? Would the pirate ship miss the rocks?

I waited and waited.

"The End," said Joe.

"What?" protested Kate. "That can't be the end.
What happened to your ship?
What happened to the pirates?
What happened to YOU?

Joe. Please tell me. Please . . ."

"I think I remember," said Joe.

I was in a barrel of fish, and then I heard a little voice.

"Welcome to the ship of Not-So-Scary Bob," muttered a clam. "He is a very strange pirate. He has never captured anyone.

I don't think he even uses cannon balls. Every day it's the same thing. Lots of noise, lots of smoke, but no results."

Just then, there was cheering from the pirates. We heard footsteps coming closer. It grew dark in the barrel.

"It's Bob!" shuddered the clam as its shell closed with a snap.

"Aha!" said Bob in a pirate voice

"I have found the little stowaway.

You are on the pirate ship of Not-So-Scary Bob. This is my ship The Rat. See my fierce rat flag?"

I looked up at the flag.

The flag was not a rat. It was a bunny with crossed carrots.

"Fierce, eh?" said Bob. "Bring me the box," he said to the crew. "I have a little surprise for our stowaway."

The pirates cheered and laughed as they brought the box.

I was scared. What was in the box? What were they going to do to me?

Bob pulled a pirate hat from the box.

"You have saved us," growled captain Bob. "You turned our ship, and we missed the rocks. Now you will be a pirate like us. Here is your pirate hat."

He put the hat on my head. I didn't know what to say, so I just smiled.

"The other ship got away," said the captain, "but that's okay. We'll try to catch it again tomorrow.

Now we must sing the pirate song, and then we will give you an eye patch," said Not-So-Scary Bob.

"The rat tattoo comes later if you're good."

We sang a song, and the pirates danced.

That afternoon, Captain Bob made many treasure maps and put them into bottles. He threw them into the ocean.

"We want lots of people to search for this treasure," he explained to me. "They will get a wonderful surprise when they open the chest!"

"Gold and jewels?" I asked him.

"No," he laughed, "I keep the gold. They get something even better - an adventure."

We sailed to an island. Bob and the pirates buried the treasure chest.

I remembered that I had been to this island a long time ago. I had seen other pirates bury boxes of gold here.

I tried to tell Bob, but he was too busy dancing with the pirates.

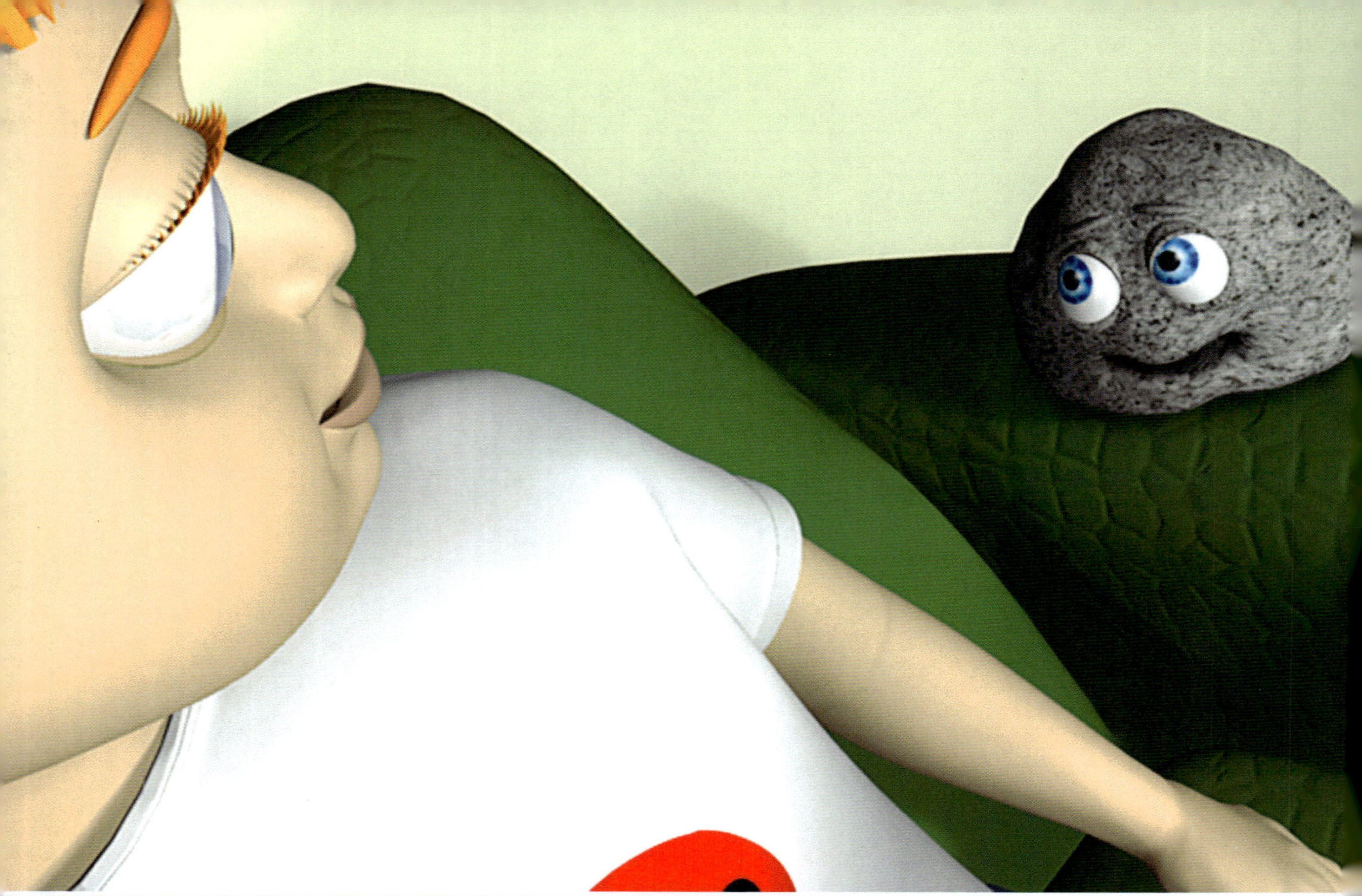

He left me to guard the treasure, and then he sailed away.

I got to keep the pirate hat!

"So I saved my ship from the pirates, and I saved the pirate ship from hitting the rocks.

That's the end of the story," said Joe. "Another time I'll tell you what was in the treasure chest."

"Is that a true story?" asked Kate.

"Mostly true," said Joe.

16326999R00017

Made in the USA
Charleston, SC
15 December 2012